He has put
his angels
in charge of you.
They will
watch over you
wherever you go.

PSALM 91:11.

Shadows and Shining Lights

Featuring G.T. and the Halo Express,
created by Doug and Debbie Kingsriter

Written by Ann Hibbard
Illustrated by Ann Neilsen

Published by Focus on the Family Publishing
Pomona, CA 91799

Distributed by Word Books, Dallas, Texas. Copyright © 1990 Focus on the Family Publishing
Scriptures quoted from *The Everyday Bible, New Century Version,* copyright © 1987, 1988 by
Word Publishing, Dallas, Texas 75039. Used by permission.
G.T. and the Halo Express, Michael, Christy and Billy Baxter
are copyrighted by Doug and Debbie Kingsriter ©1987.
No part of this book may be reproduced or copied without written permission of the publisher.

Library of Congress Catalog Card Number 90-081105
ISBN 0-929608-20-8
Cassette tapes featuring G.T. and the Halo Express in other adventures are also available by contacting King
Communications, P.O. Box 24472, Minneapolis, MN 55424 or your local Christian bookstore.

It was a perfect Friday evening, with the sky glowing a friendly pink and orange. Crickets tuned up for their night-time performance while the scent of freshly cut grass hung in the air.

"What a great night for a camp-out!" exclaimed Christy.

"Yeah," agreed her brother Michael as he stood back to admire the tent they had just put up. Buttons, their puppy, gave one of the ropes a final tug. "All the guys thought I was pretty lucky—but they bet me that I couldn't stay out the whole night."

"My friends said the same thing to me!" Christy remarked, rolling her eyes. "What do they think we are, babies?"

"Hey, we better get the flashlight and our sleeping bags—it's getting dark fast!" Christy said.

She and Michael raced across the backyard toward the brightly lit house. Buttons bounded after them, his floppy ears waving like flags in a breeze.

When they stepped back outside, the darkness seemed to swallow them up. Christy switched on the flashlight, and they peered into the black night.

"Are you sure you want to camp out, Michael?" Christy asked. "If you're scared, maybe we should just go back inside."

"Who said I was scared?" Michael responded. "Besides, do you want the whole neighborhood to laugh at us?"

"No, I guess not," Christy said.

Ever so slowly, they tiptoed toward their tent.

But Christy stumbled, stepping on Button's paw, who in turn yelped. Christy fell forward into the darkness, dropping her flashlight. It hit the ground with a thud, and the light went out.

"What happened? Where's the flashlight?" Michael asked anxiously.

"I'm trying to find it," Christy answered as her hand groped in the grass. "Here it is."

She felt for the switch. Instead of a bright, golden light, the flashlight flickered, then made only a thin, ghostly beam.

"Oh, great!" exclaimed Michael. "You broke it."

"I didn't try to trip, Michael!" Christy retorted. "What's the matter, are you scared?"

"No way—are you?"

"Of course not." Christy clutched the flashlight and slowly moved its pale beam across the shadowy backyard.

"What's that?" Michael gasped.

"What's what?" asked Christy with a frightened squeak.

"Over there," Michael whispered, pointing. "Two beady eyes!"

Christy looked hard. The longer she stared, the more she thought she saw two gleaming, yellow eyes. Was a wild animal lurking in the shadows?

A rustling noise overhead startled them. As they studied the tree, they saw frightening shapes that they had never seen in the daylight.

"Christy, do you see a face in the tree?" Michael asked in a small voice. "Isn't that a huge, bumpy nose?"

"I see a sharp claw, reaching down!" Christy's finger shook as she pointed at another part of the tree.

Buttons gave a frightened bark. Michael and Christy made a dash for the tent, almost knocking each other over as they struggled to get inside. Buttons dove between their legs and squeezed in first.

"Now we're safe," Christy announced. But she cautiously searched all the tent's corners with the fading beam of her flashlight.

Michael suddenly tensed.

"Shhh! Listen!" he hissed.

They sat perfectly still, listening to the strange night noises around them.

"Do you hear that?" Michael whispered.

"Hear what?" Christy asked. She listened hard.

The crickets screeched so loudly they sounded like millions of giant-sized insects. Trees sighed in the breeze, groaning and creaking.

Then Christy heard heavy breathing. Something wet and warm touched her ear.

Christy shrieked. Michael yelled.

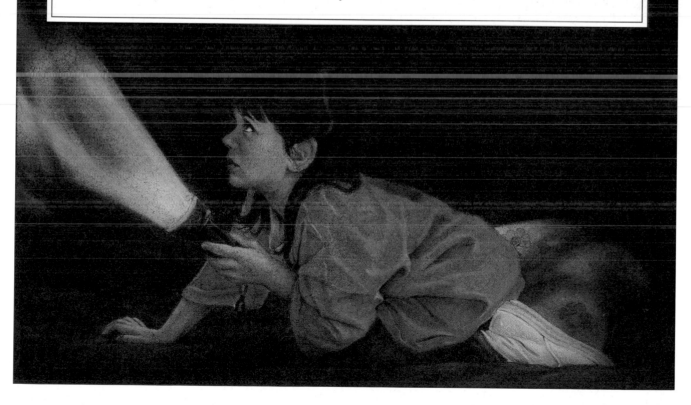

"Quit licking, Buttons! You scared us," Christy said with a giggle, petting his silky head.

They unrolled their sleeping bags and crawled inside. Just then, the flashlight blinked twice and went out.

"Oh, no," they moaned. Christy wiggled the switch, but nothing happened. The tent seemed very, very dark.

"M-m-Michael, l-l-look," Christy stammered.

All across the sides and ceiling of the tent, shadows were dancing and jerking and gliding.

Michael and Christy imagined all the horrible creatures
that might be gathered outside the tent...
    Creatures that creep and slither and slump,
    Ogres that ogle and boggle and bump,
    Monsters that mumble and bumble and crunch,
    Spiders that eat little children for lunch.

"Ooooh!" A far-away howl pierced the night.

"It's a wolf!" yelled Michael. He and Christy dove inside their sleeping bags and burrowed to the bottom.

Buttons whimpered and covered his head with his paws.

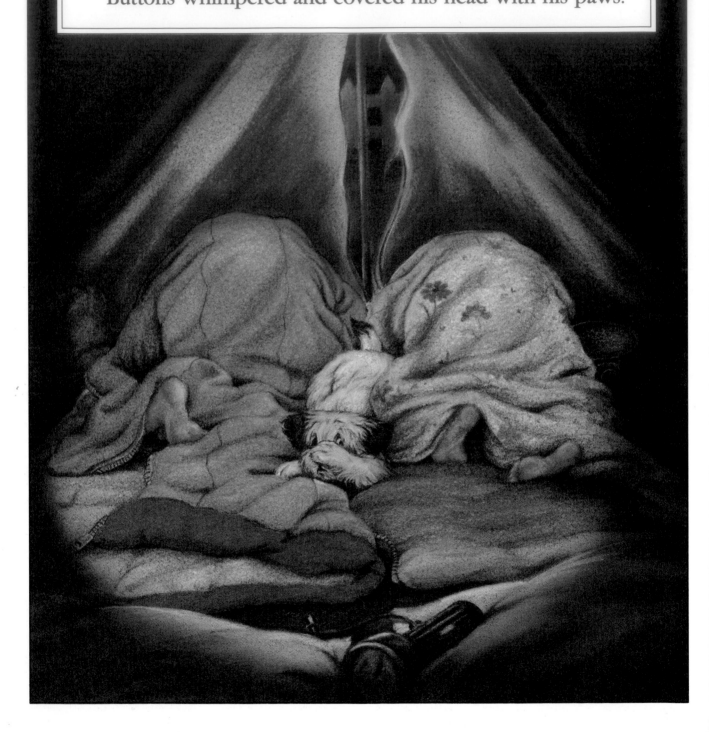

Thunk! Something landed on top of their tent.

Then they heard a friendly voice: "Hey, don't be afraid!"

Gulping with fear, Michael and Christy opened their sleeping bags just a crack and peered out.

A bright face poked through the tent flaps—upside down!

"Wh-who-who are you?" the children stammered.

Somehow, before they knew it, the stranger was sitting next to them. And he was an angel! At least he looked like an angel. He had wings and a shining white robe. But the sleeves were rolled up, and sticking out from the bottom of his robe were red tennis shoes.

"Michael and Christy, allow me to introduce myself," he said with a grin. "My name is Good Tidings, but you can call me G.T. for short. Well, hello, Buttons!"

Buttons snuggled up to G.T., closing his eyes in complete happiness.

Seeing the children's looks of amazement, G.T. continued, "I'm your guardian angel. I've been watching over you two for years. Even though you couldn't see me, I've been right there with you, helping you out of lots of scrapes. But you look a little pale."

He spread his wings around them like a big hug.

"We heard lots of scary noises," Michael blurted out, his teeth still chattering.

"We saw faces in the tree," Christy chimed in. "And monsters were dancing outside our tent!"

"Those were just the shadows of branches moving in the breeze," G.T. said with a comforting smile. "Come outside and let me show you something."

"Outside? Are you kidding?!" said Michael.

"Don't worry. I'll be with you," G.T. assured them. He gathered them up in his arms and, with a flap of his wings, whooshed them out of the tent.

They both squealed in surprise and delight.

G.T. set them down gently.

"This time, look at the light instead of the shadows," he said, a twinkle in his eye.

Michael and Christy looked up and gasped in wonder. The sky was filled with angels. Each angel held a star, and the stars spouted rays of light like a million candles.

"Oh, it's so beautiful!" Christy breathed.

Michael murmured, "Wow!"

G.T. turned to the scary, old oak tree. Perched in the branches sat angels holding musical instruments.

"This, Michael and Christy, is my band of angels, the Halo Express," G.T. announced. He picked up a fallen branch, tapped it against the tree trunk, and waved it in the air.

With that, the Halo Express began to play the most beautiful, heavenly music Michael and Christy had ever heard. Buttons joined in with a long, happy howl. The angels' music was so soft and soothing that soon the children grew sleepy.

G.T. led them back into the tent.

"Whenever you're afraid, just remember that God has sent his angels to watch over you," G.T. whispered.

"Why are angels so bright, G.T.?" asked Christy sleepily, laying her head on the pillow.

"We get our brightness from Jesus," G.T. answered. "He is the Light, and we shine because we've been with him."

G.T. hovered over them as they said their prayers and drifted off to sleep.

The next thing the children knew, the birds were chirping, and the tent was bright with morning sunlight. Michael rubbed his eyes, and Christy looked out on the dew-covered grass. Buttons scampered outside.

"Did you dream what I dreamed, Christy?" Michael asked.

"You mean about G.T. and the angels? I don't think it was a dream, Michael," said Christy.

"I wonder where they are now?" Michael mused.

Buttons looked up at the top of the tent and wagged his tail as hard as he could.